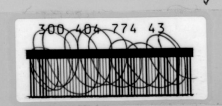

THE COBWEB CURTAIN

A Christmas Story by
Jenny Koralek

based on a legend told by
William Barclay

Illustrated by Pauline Baynes

METHUEN CHILDREN'S BOOKS

First published in Great Britain in 1989
by Methuen Children's Books
Michelin House, 81 Fulham Road,
London SW3 6RB
Illustrations copyright © 1989 by Pauline Baynes
Text copyright © 1989 by Jenny Koralek and adapted
by kind permission of The Saint Andrew Press from
The Daily Study Bible (Matthew) by William Barclay (*The
Legend of the Spider's Web*)
Printed in Belgium by Proost
ISBN 0 416 13462 9

It was cold on the night the Christ child was born. Cold in the stable,
cold in the streets, cold in the hills.

Mary, his mother, wrapped him up well and Joseph, his father, laid him in the manger full of sweet hay.

The ox and the ass stood back a little. They felt large and clumsy next to the baby, but it was their furry bodies and their steamy breath which kept the Christ child warm.

By the light of a great star three shepherds came to see the Christ child.
They did not have any presents for him because they were too poor.

Led by the same great star three wise men journeyed from far countries to see the Christ child. They brought him gold, rare herbs and perfumes. (Not much use, thought the shepherds, to anyone on a cold winter's night.)

Then the shepherds left. Of course they told everybody they met about the Christ child. And of course more people came to the stable to look into the manger. Then they went out and told others to come and see what they had seen.

The three wise men went away too, but at the gate of the city a messenger stopped them.

"Why have you come to the city of our king?" he asked. "And why did you bow down before a baby? Is he a king?"

"No," agreed the wise men.

"Not a king as we know a king," said one.

"He is the Christ child," said another.

"Sent from God," said a third.

"Oh, *really,*" said the messenger. "Where does he dwell, this special child? I am sure my king would like to bow down before him too."

"The city is not so big," said the wise men. "Your king will find the Christ child soon enough."
And they rode home swiftly and secretly by little-known paths.

The youngest shepherd had heard all that was said. Now he saw the messenger hurrying to the Palace. Suddenly he was afraid for the Christ child. He crept back to the stable.

"Come!" he whispered to Mary and Joseph. "Come with me! The child is in great danger. You must hide. Follow me and I will show you a safe place outside the city. It will be very cold and very dark, but in the morning I will bring you a donkey. Then you can ride away quickly into Egypt."

Mary snatched up the child and Joseph took her hand. They followed the shepherd down narrow streets and away from the city. He led them up into the hills to a deep, dark cave and left them there.

"Do not talk," he said. "Do not light a fire. At sunrise I will come back."

Mary held the Christ child close and Joseph put his arm round both of them. Comforted they fell asleep.

In a crack in the rock at the opening of the cave lived a spider. She heard
what the shepherd said and when he had gone she watched the mother, the
father, the child. The night was very cold. Frost was on the way and perhaps
snow, too.

"Poor things," said the spider. "What have they done to be afraid and
hiding on such a night? I cannot weave a blanket. I cannot build a door, but
I can spin a good, strong web before the frost comes."

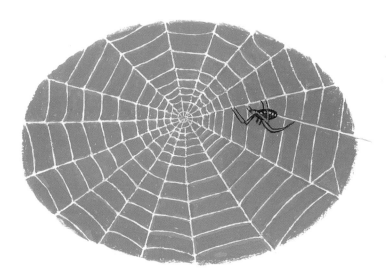

The spider began to spin as fast as she could. She spun and she spun till she had spread a web right across the opening of the cave.

Then the cruel frost came and froze the web so that it glittered in the cold moonlight.

The spider hid in her crack in the rock.

At dawn the king's soldiers came clattering up the hillside.

"What's the matter with our king?" grumbled one of them. "Sending us out on a wild chase after some poor baby?"

The spider trembled in the crack in the rock. The soldiers had stopped outside the cave.

"That's not a poor baby," said one of the soldiers. "Our king thinks this child will grow up to be a king more powerful than he is."

"Well, there's no one in there, that's for sure," said another soldier.

"How do you know without going in?" asked his companion, heavy with sleep.

"Can't you see that great spider's web all frosted and unbroken?" jeered the first soldier. "It's perfect. Frozen solid as a diamond. No. No one has been here for many days."

And they rode away to another hill far off beyond the river.

At sunrise the shepherd came back, leading a donkey. When he saw the soldiers' footprints he too trembled.

Then he saw the spider's web, how it hung like a curtain across the opening of the cave. He unfastened it very, very carefully and laid it on a small dark tree.

"Oh spider," he whispered. "Wherever you are hiding, can you hear me? This web is precious, even more precious than gold or herbs or perfumes. With it you have saved the Christ child's life."

"The Christ child?" said the spider in the crack in the rock.

"So he has come at last and for that I am glad. But had I saved the life of any child I would still be happy."

The shepherd went into the cave and led Mary and Joseph out into the light. He gave them bread and milk. Joseph lifted Mary with the Christ child in her arms onto the donkey. They thanked the shepherd in quiet voices for keeping them from harm.

As they passed the small dark tree Mary saw the spider's web.

"Look, Joseph," she said. "Look at that curtain of cobweb how it sparkles in the sun's early light."

"Yes," said Joseph. "And all the work of one small creature."

Then they rode on into Egypt while the shepherd stood and watched them until they were out of sight.

Then he dug up the small dark tree and took it home to show to his wife and children.

"That is lovely," said his wife. "Put it by the door. Is the Christ child safe?"

"Yes," said the shepherd. "Thanks to the spider who spun this web."

Together the shepherd and his family sat down by the small tree and when he had told them the whole story his children said,

"Well then! Every year on this day we must find a frosty web and hang it on a little tree to remind us of the Christ child's birthday and of what the spider did."

On Christmas Eve look at the tinsel threaded across your own dark tree.
If you turn out the lights and half close your eyes perhaps you will glimpse
the web which on that night long ago saved the Christ child's life.